FLE

Get **more** out of libraries

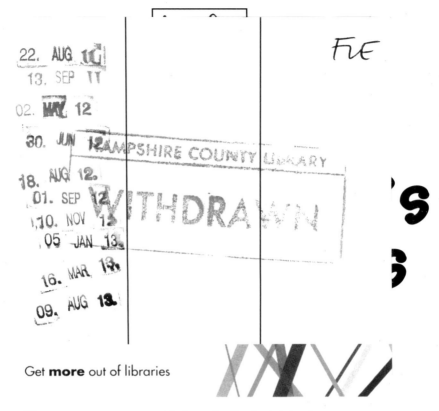

Please return or renew this item by the last date shown.
You can renew online at www.hants.gov.uk/library
Or by phoning 0845 603 5631

Hampshire
County Council

First published in 2005 by
Franklin Watts
338 Euston Road
London
NW1 3BH

Franklin Watts Australia
Level 17/207 Kent Street
Sydney
NSW 2000

A CIP catalogue record for this book is available
from the British Library.

ISBN 978 0 7496 6163 2

Series Editor: Jackie Hamley
Series Advisor: Dr Barrie Wade
Series Designer: Peter Scoulding

Printed in China

Franklin Watts is a division of
Hachette Children's Books
an Hachette Livre UK company.
www.hachettelivre.co.uk

The Emperor's New Clothes

Retold by Karen Wallace

Illustrated by François Hall

W
FRANKLIN WATTS
LONDON·SYDNEY

Once there lived an
Emperor who loved
expensive clothes.

Two men decided to cheat him. "We can make you some special cloth.

6

It's so special that stupid people cannot see it," they said.

The Emperor gave the cheats lots of money and gold thread to make the special cloth.

Soon, the Emperor came to visit the cheats' workshop. The cheats pretended to show the Emperor his cloth.

But, of course, he could see
nothing! He thought people
would call him stupid, so he
said: "What beautiful cloth!"

His courtiers couldn't see the cloth either. But no one wanted to look stupid.

So they all said: "Emperor, this cloth is the most beautiful cloth ever made!"

"Make me some new clothes by tomorrow," said the Emperor. "I will wear them for the procession!"

The cheats pretended to
cut the cloth with scissors.

Then they pretended to
sew the pieces together.

The Emperor stood
in front of a mirror.
"Here are your trousers
and coat," said the cheats.
"They are so light, you
will not feel them."

19

The cheats pretended to help the Emperor dress.

The Emperor pretended he could see his new clothes.

Everyone stared as the Emperor walked at the front of the procession.

But they all pretended they could see his new clothes.

Suddenly, a little boy shouted: "The Emperor has no clothes on!"

Everyone started to laugh.
"Look at the Emperor!
He isn't wearing
any clothes!"

The Emperor knew it
was true, but what
could he do?

He had to finish the
procession with no
clothes on!

And the cheats quickly left town with their bags full of money and gold thread!

Leapfrog has been specially designed to fit the requirements of the Literacy Framework. It offers real books for beginner readers by top authors and illustrators.

Rhyming stories are available with Leapfrog Rhyme Time.

* hardback